# MR. TURTLE'S MYSTERY

# Mr. Turtle's Mystery

Written by

BETTY MILES

Illustrated by

JACQUELINE TOMES

Alfred A. Knopf: New York

This book is for
*David Miles*

L.C. Catalog card number 60-13025

THIS IS A BORZOI BOOK,
PUBLISHED BY ALFRED A. KNOPF, INC.

# MR. TURTLE'S MYSTERY

When something happens but you don't know how, that is a mystery. Then you try to figure out what happened.

This is Mr. Turtle's mystery. But first it is necessary to tell about Mr. Turtle, himself.

**Mr.** Turtle was the best birthday present of a boy named David. "A turtle!" David said. "Hi, Mr. Turtle!" So that was his name.

Mr. Turtle was the best birthday present of a boy named David. "A turtle!" David said.

At first, Mr. Turtle looked like a little green stone with black designs and a tail. Then Mr. Turtle's head with red and yellow markings poked out of his shell, and Mr. Turtle's two bright eyes blinked up at David. Next, two legs inched out from the front of the shell, and two legs pushed out from the back.

Slowly, but very surely, the turtle began to
move straight across the table. "Hey, come
back, Mr. Turtle!" David shouted.

He picked up Mr. Turtle and set him gently in the special turtle house, which had a pool of water, a hill of bright blue pebbles, and a little green umbrella. "Stay in your safe house, Mr. Turtle," David said. "You crawl away too fast outside of it."

Each day, David learned more about Mr.
Turtle. He learned to feed him a shake from
the can of turtle food, or a tiny piece of lettuce,
or a shred of hamburger. He learned to change
the water in Mr. Turtle's house. He learned to
hold Mr. Turtle safely on the flat part of his
hand. Soon David began to call Mr. Turtle
"honey" because he began to love him.

This is how life was, with David and Mr. Turtle, before the mystery. Of course, other things happened.

David made a new friend.

He read a book about helicopters.

He learned to climb trees!

He got a new pair of tree-climbing sneakers,
and put his old brown shoes away in the closet.

But no matter what else happened, David remembered Mr. Turtle, and fed him, and changed his water, and held him gently in his hand.

And then one day, the mystery began. On this day, David played on the floor with Mr. Turtle, and watched the way he moved along the rug, and called him "honey."

What David did next is part of the mystery.
Did he put Mr. Turtle back in his house, or
did he forget to, just once?

Anyway, David left Mr. Turtle, and he went outside to climb trees.

And when David came in from his climbing,
and went to feed Mr. Turtle, Mr. Turtle was
gone!

But while David was outside, climbing very high in his tree-climbing sneakers, Mr. Turtle was in the house, moving across the rug on his small green feet.

And when David came in from his climbing,
and went to feed Mr. Turtle, Mr. Turtle was
gone!

"How *can* he be gone?" David thought first.
And then, "Where is he now?"

David began to search.

He looked under the piano,

and under the couch,

and under the table,

and all along the floor.

No Mr. Turtle.

David began to be worried. He looked on top of the table, and behind the couch pillows, and in the magazine basket—although he knew that a turtle could not get into these places by himself.

But, no matter where David looked, Mr.
Turtle was not there. So David began to hunt
in other rooms. He looked all over the kitchen.

No Mr. Turtle.

He looked in his mother's and father's room. No Mr. Turtle.

He looked in the hall, behind the dust mop and the ironing board and the vacuum cleaner. No Mr. Turtle.

And he gave a quick look inside his closet.

But he did not find Mr. Turtle. There was no Mr. Turtle to pick up and hold, and care for. Mr. Turtle was gone.

| SUN. | MON. | TUES. | WED. | THUR | FRI. | SAT. |
|------|------|-------|------|------|------|------|
|      |      |       | 1    | 2    | 3    | 4    |
| 5    | 6    | 7     | 8    | 9    | 10   | 11   |
| 12   | 13   | 14    | 15   | 16   | 17   | 18   |
| 19   | 20   | 21    | 22   | 23   | 24   | 25   |
| 26   | 27   | 28    | 29   | 30   |      |      |

This day was Saturday. On Sunday, Mr. Turtle was still gone. David found that it was hard to get used to not having a turtle, once he had got used to having one. The flat part of David's hand felt very bare, and the turtle house with the bright blue pebbles, and the green umbrella looked very empty.

David knew that a turtle can go without food and water for a fairly long time. But he worried just the same. On Monday morning, David began to tell himself that Mr. Turtle might be lost, really lost, forever.

Once or twice, he even thought about a new turtle. He thought a new one would have to be called Greenie, or Crawlie, or something like that. It could never be called Mr. Turtle. There was only one Mr. Turtle, and he was lost.

Of course, all this time, other things happened. David did a lot of climbing in his sneakers when he needed a rest from looking for his turtle.

And then, on Monday afternoon, when David ran into the house, he suddenly stopped and yelled. Because there on the floor in front of him, right in the middle of the living room rug, right out where *anyone* could see him, was—of course—

Mr. Turtle!

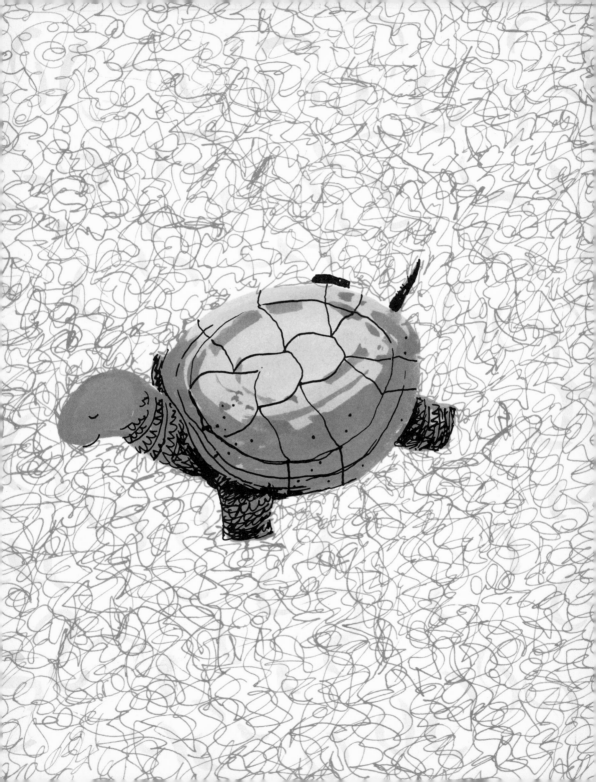

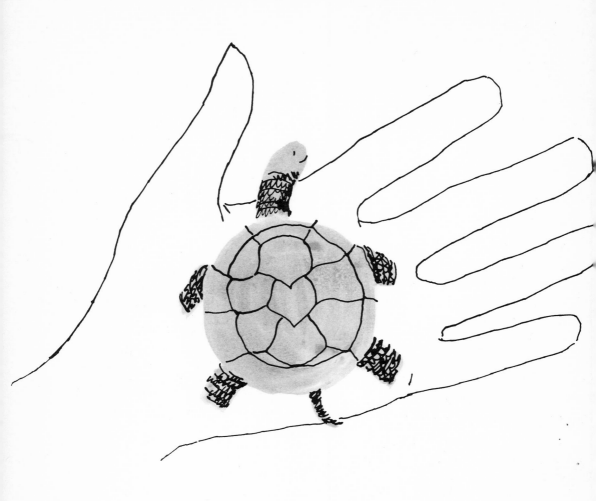

"Oh, honey," said David. "Oh, Mr. Turtle."
He held Mr. Turtle on the flat part of his
hand. Mr. Turtle stretched out his head, and
his bright little eyes blinked up at David.

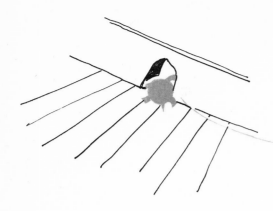

Mr. Turtle was back. But where had he been on Saturday, and on Sunday, and on Monday? David did not know, although he keeps thinking about it and guessing: In a mouse hole? Underneath the rug? Behind the refrigerator?

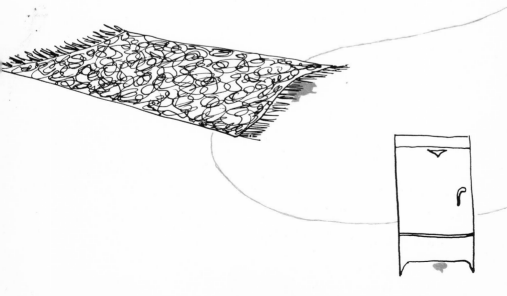

David does not know yet where Mr. Turtle
went, **and that is a mystery.**

BUT . . .

    it is not a mystery to **Mr. Turtle**.
He knew where he was all the time.

Now Mr. Turtle has a new house, with higher walls (but the same blue pebbles, and the same green umbrella) and he is always safe inside it—except for the times when he sits on the warm, gentle hand of David, who loves him.

Text set in *Fotosetter Times Roman.* Composed by *Westcott & Thomson, Phila-delphia, Pa.* Printed by *Philip Klein, New York.* Bound by *H. Wolff, New York.* Typography by *Tere LoPrete.*

# Date Due

| OCT 18 '81 | | | |
|---|---|---|---|
| MAY 23 | | | |
| DEC 2 | | | |
| | | | |
| | | | |
| | | | |
| | | | |
| | | | |
| | | | |
| | | | |
| | | | |
| | | | |
| | | | |
| | | | |
| | | | |
| | | | |
| | | | |